DATE DUE

APR 1 0 1995	
OCT 1 1 1995	
NOV 3 0 12	
APR - 4 2016	

THE BEST FIGHT

Anne Schlieper
Illustrations by Mary Beth Schwark

Albert Whitman & Company
Morton Grove, Illinois

Design by Sandy Newell.
Text is set in Clearface.

Text copyright © 1995 by Anne Schlieper.
Illustrations copyright © 1995 by Mary Beth Schwark.
Published in 1995 by Albert Whitman & Company,
6340 Oakton Street, Morton Grove, Illinois 60053.
Published simultaneously in Canada by General Publishing, Limited, Toronto.
Printed in the United States of America.
10 9 8 7 6 5 4 3 2 1

■ ■ ■

Library of Congress Cataloging-in-Publication Data
Schlieper, Anne.
The best fight / Anne Schlieper ; illustrated by Mary Beth Schwark.
p. cm.
Summary: Fifth-grader Jamie, who goes to a special class because he has difficulty reading,
thinks he's dumb until the school principal helps him realize that he also has many talents.
ISBN 0-8075-0662-1
[1. Dyslexia—Fiction. 2. Reading—Fiction.
3. Schools—Fiction. 4. Self-acceptance—Fiction.]
I. Schwark, Mary Beth, ill. II. Title.
PZ7.S34714Be   1994
[Fic]—dc20
94-8454
CIP
AC

*T*his book is for Paul and Mark, who read it first.

I am grateful to Margie Golick and Sandra Gulland for their kind and helpful appraisal of the manuscript and to John Goodman, the Director of Psychology at the Children's Hospital of Eastern Ontario, for giving this undertaking his support and encouragement.

Over the years I have been privileged to work with children who have learning disabilities. They have taught me many things about determination and bravery. I thank them all.

A. S.

CHAPTER

1

Jamie woke up smiling. He tried to keep the
wonderful feeling that was part of his dream.
Downstairs, his mother called, "Come on! You'll be
late for school!" If he could just remember—yes,
there it was—Jamie's mind reached out and caught
the dream before it melted into the morning
sunlight. He closed his eyes and coaxed back details
until it was clear and shining again.

In his dream, Jamie was reading. He was reading
a grown-up joke book. He looked at the page, and the

jokes rushed right into his mind with no effort. Just look! and there all the words were, inside his head. The jokes were about important, grownup things, and he understood them and laughed at them. The other kids stood around him and asked respectfully, "What does it say, Jamie?" He stopped reading and laughing long enough to say, "Sometime you'll learn to read, too."

For a moment, Jamie had the dream all whole and marvelous in his mind. Then he remembered what really had happened yesterday. The dream slid away forever, and he felt his old, familiar burden settle over him.

Jamie tried not to think about yesterday, but he couldn't help it. He saw again the little knot of kids in the corner of the yard—Sean and Jason and David and Stu, his friends from Ms. McLaughlin's fifth-grade homeroom. They were handing around a book and taking turns reading it. They were off in a corner and sort of huddled over the book. From the way they laughed, Jamie knew it was about grownup things.

"Hey, guys!" Jamie called. "What've you got there? What's so funny?"

They looked at him a bit uncertainly. "It's my big brother's joke book," Jason explained. "We're taking turns reading the jokes."

Sean broke in. "Look, Jamie, butt out, will you? We're reading." Jamie knew what was coming. It was what they had always teased him about, ever since first grade. "Jamie's a baby!" "Jamie can't read!" "Jamie can't spell 'cat!' " "Jamie is a dum-dum!" Most of the time he just tried to shrug and yell something back, but it always hurt.

And sometimes it *really* hurt. Right now, he wanted so much to be with those kids and read the grownup jokes and laugh along with them in that knowing way. He was ten, nearly eleven, for Pete's sake. He was growing up, and they were trying to shut him out of the grown-up stuff. He felt tears behind his eyes, and he panicked. Anything was better than crying!

So he shoved Sean and grabbed the book from Jason and threw it at David. All the time he was yelling, "You're a bunch of lousy freaks! I don't care about your stupid jokes!" And then everyone was hitting and scuffling until the teacher on yard duty came rushing up, shouting, "Principal's office! Principal's office!"

Next thing, there they were in a row on the bench outside the office, trying not to meet the eyes of any of the kids in the hall. Jamie and Sean turned to each other and muttered, "Sorry," at the same moment, and then they grinned at each other. So that was all right. Stu and David slid grins toward Jamie, too.

But Jason stayed mad. He leaned across Sean and whispered to Jamie, "You started it! You got us all in trouble, you dum-dum." He was going to go on, but Sean mumbled, "Shut up! Here comes Old Wilson."

Of course, Old Wilson gave them all detentions and a little talk about not fighting. He kept Jamie back as the others left. Then he said quietly, "I seem to be seeing a lot of you, young James. I think next time you turn up at my door I'll have to have a talk with your parents."

Oh, great! Pretty soon his parents would hear from Old Wilson because, of course, he would fight again. Especially now, with Jason mad at him. Jason would go on and on, calling him "baby" and "dummy" until he had to fight. Then his mom and dad would hear about it, and his mom would cry and say, "Oh Jamie, why do you do it?" and he couldn't tell her. He could never explain to her how awful he felt about not reading. That was the secret part of his burden, the worst part. He couldn't even imagine talking about that part with anyone . . .

But here it was, the day after, and Jamie had to go to school. He shuffled downstairs, dragging his book bag and hoping no one would talk to him at breakfast. What was the point of having happy dreams, anyway? They just made you feel worse when you woke up and remembered.

CHAPTER

Every morning after recess, Jamie went to his
special teacher for reading and spelling. He went
there while the fifth grade was doing real reading and
spelling. Another kid, Kenny, went along with him.
That's how it had been since first grade. Every year
he and Kenny were in the same homeroom. Every
morning of every year they got up and walked out as
soon as their real teacher said, "Take out your
readers, class." Jamie and Kenny would try to look as
if they didn't care. They always whispered and

scuffled going down the hall. They never exactly looked at each other because who wants to look at a friend when he's feeling embarrassed? They both understood that, even though they never talked about it.

That's strange, Jamie thought. *We've been going out to Special Class forever, and we don't even let on to each other that we go there.* It was a new thought, and Jamie wasn't sure he liked it. Why think about things like that? If you started wondering about the way things were done, you could end up with no friends at all. He'd seen it happen to other guys, but not him! He checked to see that there weren't any teachers around. Then he jabbed Kenny in the ribs and ran the last few steps to the Special classroom.

There was one good thing about the kids in Special Class: they kept their heads down when anyone was reading out loud. They never made fun afterwards, either. Reading in Special Class was a lot better than trying to read in real class. Back in first grade, Jamie remembered, before they put him into Special Class, he cried every day. Of course, he was just a baby then, but it had been so awful he could make himself shivery just thinking about it. He'd expected to learn to read the very first day of first grade. That was a laugh! Instead of learning to read, he'd spent months and months getting more and more ashamed and mixed up, and never getting anything right. He remembered how his friends were all reading their first-grade readers. He used to watch them to see what they did, but they never seemed to do anything special. They just looked at the page and said words. He looked at the page and said words, too, but they were almost always the wrong words. After awhile, the kids would start to laugh as soon as the teacher said, "It's your turn to read, Jamie." It was the worst time in his whole life.

"Daydreaming again, Jamie?" Ms. Clayton, his special teacher, had stopped beside his chair. "You won't make progress that way! Here, read this page out loud, and I'll help you with the hard words."

Jamie read slowly. He followed the words with his finger, and he sounded out some of them. " 'Jim had a good birthday present,' " he read. " 'It was a dirt bike. He rode it on the grass. He had a lot of fun, and he fell off just once.' " He got all the words right except "birthday." That was his kind of reading: slow, slow. He worked so hard at it that after a few lines, he felt more tired than after an hour of hockey practice. The kids in real fifth grade still just looked at their real books and knew all the right words without even trying. That kind of reading was never going to happen to him.

"Great, Jamie, just great!" Ms. Clayton was saying

heartily. "You're doing great work. Keep it up!"

She says that to all of us, no matter how we read, Jamie realized suddenly. *She doesn't even notice she's saying it.* Ms. Clayton was a new teacher, and she was okay. She was always cheerful. Nothing seemed to make her mad, and she could think of all kinds of fun things to do in the last ten minutes every day. *But,* Jamie thought, *if she says "great" to everyone all the time, it's like not saying it at all. Maybe she never really means it.*

All at once, Jamie knew he wanted to give up. He pushed his book away and said, "This is dumb! I hate it! I'll never learn to read!"

Kenny and the other kids got very quiet. Jamie was breaking the rule: you came to this dum-dum class and did the work, and all the time you pretended you weren't really here. The silence waited for him to say something more. Into the silence he

said, "I want to read real stuff! Why can't I learn to read the real readers?"

Then he looked up and met Ms. Clayton's eyes. Ms. Clayton was just as still as the kids were. She was looking kind of frozen, almost as if she felt scared. That expression made Jamie feel really sorry he'd ever said anything. "Oh, forget it," he mumbled. He pulled his book back toward him and looked at Ms. Clayton and the other kids. "I'm sorry. I. . . I didn't mean it."

Then everyone moved and fiddled with their books, and Ms. Clayton unfroze and gave Jamie her big smile. "That's okay, Jamie. We all feel low sometimes. But no more talk about giving up, right? We don't talk that way here! Besides, you're doing great! Just great!" Ms. Clayton gave him another big grin and moved along to look at another kid's work, and that was that. Just one more dumb thing he'd done in a week that had gone wrong from the start.

But why had Ms. Clayton looked scared? Jamie tried to puzzle it out. Could Ms. Clayton be pretending, the same as the kids? Could she be saying, "Great, great," and all the time be telling herself that she wasn't there, either? For some reason that thought made Jamie feel so lonely he couldn't bear it. He made the thought go away fast.

Ms. Clayton wasn't scared, he told himself. *She was just mad at me. I'll work real hard tomorrow to show her I didn't mean it. And when she says, "Great, great," I'll pretend I believe her.*

CHAPTER

3

Even the worst weeks finally get to Friday and finish themselves off. On Saturday morning, hockey practice started at 10:30, and everything was all right again.

Jamie was always happy on Saturday mornings. After breakfast, he went down the street to get Steven, his very best friend, and they went on to the rink together. Steven had lived on the block ever since he was born, and he and Jamie had been friends right from the start. They began school in the same kindergarten. But then Steven had taken some kind of test that showed he could learn faster than almost anyone. So now he went to a different school where they taught everything faster than normal.

Steven's parents said that he went to the other school because he was gifted. That word made Steven so embarrassed that Jamie never used it. Sometimes Steven brought home pages of riddles, puzzles, and brainteasers from his school. He read them to Jamie, and they figured them out together. Jamie thought those pages were fun, and he didn't mind that Steven read to him. Steven always helped him without rubbing it in. He was the best friend a person could have.

Steven played hockey pretty well, too, but not as well as Jamie. Jamie was the best player on the team. When Jamie was on the ice, everything was easy. He just thought what he wanted to do, and he did it.

This was his third winter with the team, and he knew all the plays so well he felt he'd always known them. When he had the puck, he hardly ever lost it. When he shot, the puck went true. He could skate so fast he even surprised himself sometimes.

The coach really liked the way he played. Jamie could tell because after practice, as they swung up off the ice, the coach would say a word or two to each of them. "Work on your stick handling, Sean." "Not so much body checking, Jason." And so on. Every now and then he'd just tap someone on the shoulder and say, "Good playing." That's what he nearly always said to Jamie—"Good playing, Jamie." It made a lot of the dumb school stuff stop hurting for a while.

After hockey practice, Jamie and Steven always went over to the shopping center and spent most of their allowances on hamburgers. Then they roamed around the mall, checking out the interesting stores, like the sports shop and the pet store. Today, there were puppies in the pet store window. They wriggled and tumbled and looked up with pleased expressions. *They're so happy,* Jamie thought. *But maybe they'll leave the store and have bad luck in their lives.* He hated these sad thoughts that came creeping into his mind, but he couldn't make them go away.

"Steven," he blurted out, "Steven, how did you learn to read?" The minute the words were said he wished he hadn't said them, but Steven didn't seem surprised or embarrassed.

He spoke slowly, thinking it out. "It's hard to remember. I know I could read in kindergarten. I asked my mom about it once, and she told me I learned the letters from 'Sesame Street,' and I used to ask her what words said, like on signs and T-shirts and stuff, and after awhile I just knew how to read. It wasn't really learning, like studying science or

something. It just happened."

Jamie stared at the foolish, hopeful puppies. *It just happened,* he thought. *It just happened, but it never happened to me. There's something wrong with my head where reading should be. I'll never, ever learn.* The puppies got all blurred and shimmery. *Don't cry,* he told himself desperately. *Don't cry.*

Out loud he said, "Oh well, I just wondered. It doesn't matter. Let's go look at the video games. We've watched these dumb dogs long enough!" He ran down the corridor, dodging shoppers, Steven trailing behind. They spent their last money playing a neat new outer space game.

CHAPTER

4

Monday morning on the way to school, Jamie remembered how mad Jason had been after the fight. Why hadn't Jason tried to get even? Maybe the other kids had talked him out of it. Anyway, it was a long time ago now; Jason must have forgotten about it.

At recess, Jason and the other kids were off in a corner of the playground, just like the day of the fight. This time, though, Jason called, "Hey, Jamie, come here! We're planning something." He held out an envelope. "It's an invitation to my birthday party."

Jamie felt confused. Why were the other kids so quiet and watching him so hard? Maybe they wanted to see if he was still mad at Jason. They were all waiting for something.

He took the envelope and opened it up. There was a card with a picture of balloons and presents on the front. He opened it and saw his name, but he couldn't read the rest—it would take too long, and the kids were waiting. It must be okay. "Well, thanks, Jason," he said at last.

"It's all right, then?" Jason insisted. "Everything's fine with you?"

Jamie didn't understand this, but he couldn't back out now. "Sure Jason, just fine," he said uneasily. "Thanks again."

Then some of the kids burst out laughing, and Jason snatched back the card. "Listen, you dummy!" he yelled. "Listen to what you thanked me for!

'Jamie is too stupid to learn anything! Jamie's the dumbest kid in the whole school! Jamie's a freak—' "

That was as far as he got because Jamie had him down on the ground and was punching him again and again, blotting out the hateful words. Jason was winded and scared and hardly fighting back. The other kids had stopped laughing. They better have stopped! No one better laugh at him ever again!

"Jamie!" That was Sean, sounding really frightened. "Jamie, cut it out! It was just a joke!" Someone was tugging at Jamie. He punched Jason some more.

Then a grown-up voice broke in: the yard teacher, of course. Reality came back, and Jamie knew that he was in deep trouble. "James, stop that at once! Come with me! I'm reporting you to Mr. Wilson!"

Jason was picking himself up, and no one was talking to him. The other kids hung back while the yard teacher marched him away. "I'm sorry, Jamie!" Sean shouted. Well, that was something.

Jamie was back again on the long bench outside Mr. Wilson's office. All alone this time, and in the worst trouble of his life.

How could he have fallen for Jason's stupid trick? Jason wouldn't try it again, though! *I'm glad I pounded him,* Jamie thought. *I don't care what happens to me. I'm glad I did it.* But he didn't feel glad. He felt terrible. Old Wilson was sure to tell his mom and dad, and he'd probably think up some awful punishment, as well. Would Old Wilson expel him? Would he call the police? Jamie hunched over with misery.

The yard teacher came out of Mr. Wilson's office, looking smug. "The principal will see you now," she said in an icy voice.

Jamie dragged himself up and shuffled into the

office. He looked at the floor. He just couldn't look at Old Wilson and see the anger that must be in his eyes.

"James—Jamie,"—the voice was low and quiet—"I know it's hard for you to read. I know you fight because the other boys tease you. I've known that all along."

Oh, that quiet, kind voice, saying things that couldn't be said! It made the worst happen, the very worst. Jamie burst into tears. He cried out loud, like a baby. All the sad thoughts of the past week just burst out into those loud, shaming sobs. He turned away; he wanted to disappear. Could they hear him out in the hall? He wanted to die.

Mr. Wilson's voice again, brisk and businesslike this time: "Tissues on my desk, Jamie. I have to step out for a minute. Wait for me here—we have some talking to do." A firm hand on his shoulder, then the door clicked open and shut.

Jamie used a tissue. He managed to stop bawling out loud. He blew his nose some more, and after awhile he knew he'd finished crying. He stumbled over to a chair and waited for Old Wilson.

CHAPTER

5

A few minutes later, Mr. Wilson came in,
dumped some papers on his desk, and pulled a chair
up close to Jamie's. "I'm not going to ask you why
you've been getting into one fight after another
lately. Instead I'm going to tell you . . . to tell you . . .
your story, the way I see it." He spoke slowly,
choosing his words. "You've carried a burden, Jamie,
ever since you started school, because you've had to
work so hard at your reading. The only times you feel
really fine and carefree are the times when you can

forget all about reading. But it gets harder to forget as you get older, doesn't it? You're beginning to wonder what sort of person you'll grow up to be. And the thought that you might never be able to read well is really scary." He paused and looked right at Jamie. "How am I doing? Have I got it right so far?"

There was a long, waiting silence. Jamie stared out of the window at some kids who were practicing soccer. Finally he half-nodded, half-shrugged. Got it right! Old Wilson must be reading his mind! He was almost afraid to listen. What would that careful voice pull out of his mind next?

Mr. Wilson leaned forward on his desk and spoke quietly. "You can't put it away and be free of it anymore. You don't see any way of fighting against your burden, so you fight anyone who reminds you of it. But that doesn't help, because the burden never gets any lighter, no matter how much you fight the other guys. Is that how it's been?"

Another silence. Finally, Jamie muttered, "Yeah, sort of."

"Okay." Mr. Wilson's voice was brisk again. "So I *do* have it straight. That's good. You've been fighting in the dark, haven't you? Well, here's your punishment. You'll come to my office for detentions every day for a week, and we'll talk about this burden of yours. You may decide it's not so mysterious and hopeless after all." He chuckled. "You can tell the guys I'm lecturing you about fighting. You're a brave fighter, Jamie, and I respect that. I'll try to help you fight that burden instead of beating up the other guys."

He stood up. "I'll see you tomorrow."

Jamie got as far as the door. "Mr. Wilson . . . do you have to tell my mom and dad?"

"Yes, Jamie, I do. But I'll ask them to let us work

this out together. Now, you'd better get back to class. Be here tomorrow."

Jason wasn't around after school, and Jamie shrugged away from the other kids. "I just got detentions," he said. He walked slowly down his own familiar street, shivering because he was tired from fighting and crying and trying not to cry. His worst day was still happening. He had to face his mom and dad.

Warmth and the good smell of dinner cooking met him as he opened the front door. *Maybe I can sneak in,* he thought. But habit made him shout, "Hi, mom, I'm home!" and wander into the kitchen.

One look told him that Old Wilson had already phoned and his mom had been crying. She gazed at him steadily. "Mr. Wilson called. He told me you'd been in some trouble, and you'd have detentions. Jamie, he especially asked me to leave it all to him—

'school business,' he called it, 'between James and me'—so I promised him I would." She paused, then smiled her ordinary, welcome-home smile. "You're cold! I'll make some hot chocolate. You go watch your show while I get a good snack together."

Jamie's world came back into focus. He was safe at home, and his mom and dad would never know the worst of that black afternoon. He curled up on the couch in front of the TV and felt his shivering stop and warmth creep over him. He was asleep before his snack was ready.

CHAPTER

6

Jamie didn't know what to expect on the first detention day. How could anyone make things better for him? Still, Mr. Wilson seemed so sure that they had important things to talk about . . .

"Jamie, you're really intelligent. You think clearly, and you reason well. That's the first thing you should know. Anyone who knows you well can see that you're smart. But if you want proof—well, you know our psychologist did tests of your intelligence. Every time, you came out smarter than most kids your age."

Jamie couldn't let him say that. "How can I be smart when I can't read? The smart kids are like my friend Steven. They learn to read without even trying!"

"That's true, Jamie. Most smart kids do learn to read without trying very hard. But it doesn't always work out that way. Sometimes our brains let us learn some things easily and make us work really hard to learn other things. You've been able to learn most things pretty easily, haven't you?"

Jamie didn't answer for a long time. He'd never thought much about things he was good at; the reading burden made everything else seem unimportant. "Well," he said slowly, "I'm okay at science. Math's easy except for reading the problems, and I can do a bunch of stuff on the computer . . ." His voice trailed off; he was remembering that sometimes he even got the answers to puzzles before

Steven did. "Yeah," he said, "I guess I'm good at some things."

Mr. Wilson was leafing through some papers on his desk. "These are copies of all your reports, Jamie. Your math has always been good, and your teacher says you're showing a real talent for science. I'll bet your mom and dad feel proud of the way you can learn!"

"No!" Jamie didn't want to say it, but it burst out. "Not my dad! In first grade he yelled at me all the time! He doesn't yell anymore, but I know he thinks I'm dumb." He wished he hadn't said that. He felt as if he'd said something bad about his father. Besides, there was nothing Mr. Wilson could do about the sadness between him and his dad, the feeling that he'd let his dad down by not being able to read.

Mr. Wilson didn't answer right away. He moved some papers around on his cluttered desk. Then he

pushed them to one side and cleared his throat.
"Let me tell you about a talk I had with your father, "
he said. "It was a long time ago, when you were just
finishing first grade. We knew you'd had an unhappy
year, and we *were* worried about you. But I
remember your father telling me what a smart little
guy you were. 'Whatever his problem is,' your dad
said, 'it's not a lack of brains. He's just as sharp as
can be about most things.' He's said the same kind
of thing at every parent-teacher night ever since.
Believe me, Jamie, your dad has always been proud
of you."

Jamie didn't answer. He didn't want to talk about
his father anymore; it didn't feel right. Besides, he
needed to think for a long time about those words,
"Whatever his problem is, it's not a lack of brains."
Had his dad really said that, way back when Jamie
was in first grade?

That evening, Montreal was playing Chicago. When a game was on, Jamie was allowed to watch the first period, but then he had to go to bed. Sometimes, if a game was really important, his dad would wake him up and tell him the final score.

Play had just started when his father came in and sat down beside him. That was the way they usually talked, sitting side by side and watching something. When he was a baby, Jamie used to hold his father's hand while they sat together. Now that he was big, he didn't do that anymore unless he needed to.

After awhile, his father cleared his throat and glanced over at him. "Your mother tells me you're seeing the principal this week. What does he have to say?"

Jamie stared at the game while Montreal got a power play going. Could he risk it? He had to. "He says I'm smart. He says *you* think I'm smart!" He held his breath; maybe saying that was a big mistake.

It seemed forever before his father answered. At last he said softly, "Of course I think you're smart, Jamie. You are smart. Everyone knows that." He was quiet for a while. "I guess I never told you, but I couldn't read too well in school, either. I didn't have as much trouble as you, but it was always hard for me. I got teased, and I fought, just the way you do."

"It was hard?" said Jamie. "You had to fight?" He couldn't have heard it right. "Like me?"

His dad sighed. "Just like you, Jamie. We're both fighters, aren't we? I fought my way through school, and after awhile I learned to read well enough, but I always thought I was dumb. Even when I grew up and got a good job, I thought I was just lucky. I never thought of myself as smart."

"You *are* smart!" Jamie burst out. "You know just about everything!"

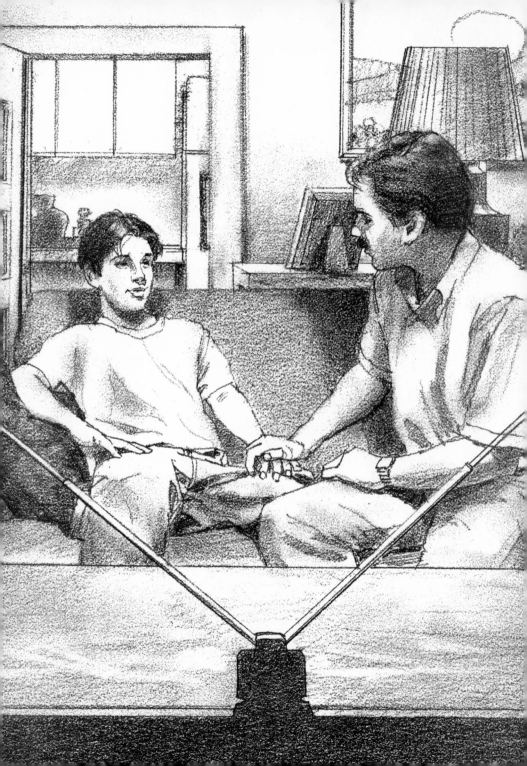

His dad smiled. "It feels good to hear that, but you're old enough to realize there are a few things I don't know! And lots of times I don't feel that smart, either!"

Jamie turned back to the screen. The puck was tied up in the Chicago end. He watched till it cleared down the ice, but he wasn't thinking about the game. "Why didn't you tell me before?"

His dad rubbed his forehead. He always did that when he was thinking hard. "I felt so badly for you, Jamie. I felt it was my fault, somehow, that you were having the same trouble I did. That's why I never said much about it. Maybe that was wrong. . . Anyway, I knew you weren't dumb! You picked up everything but reading so fast I could hardly believe it. And that made me realize that perhaps I'm not so dumb, either."

He reached out for Jamie's hand and held it tight.

"Let's both give ourselves some credit, okay? We're two smart people, doing our best."

Jamie couldn't find words for what he felt. He squeezed his dad's hand hard. The first period swept to a scoreless finish, and his dad stretched and grinned, then reached over and hugged him. "I don't know about you, but this feels like a special night to me. Go ask your mother if you can stay up for the whole game!"

CHAPTER

The rest of detention week all ran together when Jamie thought about it afterwards. He remembered how carefully Mr. Wilson had listened to all his questions. And he could hear Mr. Wilson's quiet voice, answering, explaining, not letting go of an idea until he was sure that Jamie understood.

Jamie'd asked a lot of questions, and sometimes he even argued with Mr. Wilson. He tried to remember everything so he could think about it while he walked home. His mom and dad didn't ask him anything more about his detentions, and he didn't tell them anything. *Someday I'll tell them,* he thought. He didn't say anything to the other kids, of course, except for Steven.

Some of the things Mr. Wilson said were easy to remember. "You learn most things well, Jamie. But there is one important thing you can't learn as easily as most kids your age, and that's reading. You have a reading disability."

Jamie sighed. "I know. I've heard that crummy word before."

Mr. Wilson nodded. "It's a kind of heavy word," he said, "but it's the right word for a heavy burden. You know how heavy it is. I wouldn't insult you by trying to say it's small or unimportant."

Jamie *did* feel hurt by that word, 'disability.' It had always sounded so bad to him, like a sickness that would never go away. But Mr. Wilson explained that it was a short way of saying that something was very, very hard to do.

"The way I see it, learning to read is a lot like learning to talk for most kids. After all, reading is seeing language instead of hearing it! I think brains must have a special way of learning reading. You could call it a reading advantage, an extra something that favors learning to read. Does that make sense?"

Jamie thought of his friends looking at their books, saying all the right words in first grade. "It was like that for the other kids, but not for me."

Mr. Wilson nodded. "Well, that's where your 'disability' comes in. Quite a few people—maybe one in ten, and you're one of them, Jamie—don't have that extra advantage. They have to learn to read the way they'd tackle any other hard, complicated learning job. Does that sound like you?"

Did it! "Reading is harder than anything!" Jamie

thought for a moment. "Except maybe piano lessons, but I didn't have to keep on taking them." He stopped again because his voice had gone funny. "People *have* to read."

Mr. Wilson didn't seem to notice the quaver in Jamie's voice. He was fiddling with a paperweight on his desk, the kind that made snow when it was turned upside down. He turned it and they both watched while the snow swirled and cleared. Then he looked up with a smile. "You can learn to read, Jamie, and you are learning. But you're doing it without any extra favors from your brain. You missed out on that built-in advantage. You're doing it the hard way."

That night, Jamie tried to explain things to Steven. "He says my brain doesn't know reading is special. Most people's brains do know, and that helps them learn. He says it's a reading advantage. I don't have an advantage, and that's why it's hard for me."

Jamie thought he'd made a mess of explaining, but Steven was nodding as if it made sense. "Hey," he said, "I like that! I always wondered how I learned to read when I was so little. I mean"—he grinned,— "I'm not *that* brilliant! I have to *work* to be brilliant at most things. Tell me what he says next; Old Wilson knows some neat stuff!"

But Jamie kept quiet about the next thing Mr. Wilson talked about. "You always say you can't read, but that's not exactly true, is it? You couldn't read a single word in first grade. But now you can read most of the things second- and third-grade kids read."

"What good is that?" Jamie argued. "I'm in *fifth* grade! I'm still miles behind everybody else."

"Sure, it's slow compared to your friends, but you *are* learning. Your good brain is carrying you ahead in reading just as fast as it can without that extra advantage."

Jamie didn't tell Steven because he felt embarrassed. Reading like a third grader wasn't much when Steven could read like a grownup. But Mr. Wilson was right, it *was* reading. Next time he and Steven did a puzzle, he didn't give it to Steven right away; he looked at it first and tried to read the directions. Steven knew what he was doing, but that was okay; he didn't mind Steven seeing him try. And he was surprised how many words he could read when he sounded them out.

One day, Jamie and Mr. Wilson talked about fighting. "I *have* to fight," Jamie said. "I can't let the guys hassle me. If I let them do it, they won't be my friends anyway." How could he make Mr. Wilson understand? Everything must have been so different long ago when Mr. Wilson was a kid.

Mr. Wilson smiled sympathetically. "I know you've been teased a lot, and I know you have to do something about it, but fighting's not the best answer. Want to hear about my one-two punch for handling teasing?"

"Okay, sure." But something that worked when Mr. Wilson was a kid wasn't going to help him with Jason and the others.

"Just two parts to it. One—admit whatever you're being teased about. Two—tease them back about something else. Try it! The first part takes the sting out of their teasing, and the second part hurts their feelings a little. Then it's no fun for them!"

It sounded as if it might work after all.

That night, Jamie talked to Steven about it. "Mr. Wilson told me a good put-down," he said. "But I'm not going to tell you what it was. Someday I'll use it on you!"

Steven laughed and gave him a shove. "I'm not scared! I can put down your put-down any time!"

They wrestled till they were out of breath and Steven's mom called, "That's enough, boys!"

Finally, Friday came. Mr. Wilson ended the last detention day with words that Jamie kept for his own and never told anyone: "You think of yourself as a fighter, and you have got a fight on your hands, Jamie, a long, hard one. It's the fight to learn and succeed and be the best you can be, with no extra advantage, no extra favor. That's one worth fighting, Jamie! The best fight of all."

Mr. Wilson stood up and held out his hand. "I think we've said some good things to each other, Jamie. Come and see me if you want to talk some more."

Jamie surprised himself; he was feeling sorry that the week was over. He wished he could say something important, but all he could think of as he shook Mr. Wilson's hand was, "Thanks."

CHAPTER

8

Jamie's detentions were over. Everything was the same as ever, and yet not quite the same. For one thing, he didn't wake up thinking about his burden. Instead, Mr. Wilson's words were waiting for him every morning, ready to leap into his mind in an exciting jumble—"intelligent . . . no extra advantage . . . one—two punch . . . long, hard fight . . ." Jamie wasn't sure how well he understood all those ideas, but they made him feel strong and ready to face hard things.

For another thing, Jamie found himself thinking new thoughts in Special Class: *I can read some, I've learned a lot since first grade,* and even *I've done pretty well without any extra advantage.* No one noticed anything different about him. Ms. Clayton still said, "Great, just great!" no matter what anyone did. Jamie started to take his reader home at night and practice reading when he was alone in his room. He didn't tell anyone about that.

One day, listening to Ms. Clayton's "Great, just great," Jamie realized, *I don't need anyone to tell me how I've done. I know if I've done okay or not. I can tell myself.*

Then he remembered his coach saying, "Good playing, Jamie," and Mr. Wilson saying, "You're a brave fighter." *I still like it best,* he thought, *when someone says a good thing and really means it.*

Then there was the day in gym class when the

teacher said, "I'm going to teach you a new relay game. It has quite a few rules, so I'll hand around instruction sheets. I want you to read them while I set up."

Jamie took a sheet from the stack that was going around. Jason came up to him and said, just loud enough so the others could hear, "Going to read us the instructions, Jamie?" and looked around with a grin, making sure everyone got the joke.

Jamie turned and stared at him. *Jason's just silly,* he thought. *He teases so much, like a little kid. He gets boring.* Out loud he said, "But I can't read, Jason. I thought you knew that! You should try to remember—maybe your memory's bad!"

There was a little silence. Would Mr. Wilson's one-two punch work? Maybe he shouldn't have tried it with Jason. Then he heard the other kids snickering—laughing at Jason! They were laughing

at Jason! He'd done it! Jamie didn't even feel mad. He joined in the laughter.

Jason crumpled up his instruction sheet and threw it down. "All right over there," the gym teacher shouted, "let's get going!"

Jamie walked on air all day. It'd really worked! What a weapon! Every time he remembered Jason's face, he laughed some more inside.

CHAPTER

Jamie was dreaming. In his dream, he was fighting his way through a tangled, moonlit forest. He slashed at the branches with his long, sharp sword, and as he slashed they turned into dark, towering letters that fell and formed words on the pale ground. He trudged on, striking the dreadful dark tangled letters and leaving behind him a path of tame, neat lines of print. His arm ached, his eyes stung, but all he felt was the joy of fighting and winning. The other kids were ahead of him, beyond the forest. They were saying, "Jamie's a real fighter," "Jamie's going through the hardest part," "Jamie can do it . . ."

The dream voices faded, and his mother was calling, "Jamie, time to get up!" Jamie caught his dream just before it melted into the sunlight and held it, perfect and shining, in his mind. *The best fight of all,* he thought, *and it's one I can win.*

"Jamie," his mother called, "come on!"

March 3, 1995